Dear Parents:

Congratulations! Your child is taking the first steps on an exciting journey. The destination? Independent reading!

STEP INTO READING® will help your child get there. The program offers five steps to reading success. Each step includes fun stories and colorful art or photographs. In addition to original fiction and books with favorite characters, there are Step into Reading Non-Fiction Readers, Phonics Readers and Boxed Sets, Sticker Readers, and Comic Readers—a complete literacy program with something to interest every child.

Learning to Read, Step by Step!

Ready to Read   Preschool–Kindergarten
• big type and easy words • rhyme and rhythm • picture clues
For children who know the alphabet and are eager to begin reading.

Reading with Help   Preschool–Grade 1
• basic vocabulary • short sentences • simple stories
For children who recognize familiar words and sound out new words with help.

Reading on Your Own   Grades 1–3
• engaging characters • easy-to-follow plots • popular topics
For children who are ready to read on their own.

Reading Paragraphs   Grades 2–3
• challenging vocabulary • short paragraphs • exciting stories
For newly independent readers who read simple sentences with confidence.

Ready for Chapters   Grades 2–4
• chapters • longer paragraphs • full-color art
For children who want to take the plunge into chapter books but still like colorful pictures.

STEP INTO READING® is designed to give every child a successful reading experience. The grade levels are only guides; children will progress through the steps at their own speed, developing confidence in their reading. The F&P Text Level on the back cover serves as another tool to help you choose the right book for your child.

Remember, a lifetime love of reading starts with a single step!

Copyright © 2015 by Random House LLC

All rights reserved. Published in the United States by Random House Children's Books, a division of Random House LLC, a Penguin Random House Company, New York. This work is adapted from *Everything Happens to Aaron in the Spring* by P. D. Eastman, copyright © 1967 and renewed 1995 by Random House LLC. The artwork herein originally appeared in *Everything Happens to Aaron in the Spring* and *The Cat in the Hat Beginner Book Dictionary. The Cat in the Hat Beginner Book Dictionary* by the Cat himself and P. D. Eastman, copyright © 1964 and renewed 1992 by Random House LLC.

Step into Reading, Random House, and the Random House colophon are registered trademarks of Random House LLC.

Visit us on the Web!
StepIntoReading.com
randomhousekids.com

Educators and librarians, for a variety of teaching tools, visit us at RHTeachersLibrarians.com

Library of Congress Cataloging-in-Publication Data
Eastman, P. D. (Philip D.)
Aaron is a good sport / P. D. Eastman.
   pages cm. — (Step into reading. Step 1 reader)
Summary: "Aaron the Alligator loves to play sports—but isn't quite an all-star athlete." —Provided by publisher.
ISBN 978-0-553-50842-0 (pbk.) — ISBN 978-0-375-97409-0 (lib. bdg.) — ISBN 978-0-553-50843-7 (ebook)
[1. Ability—Fiction. 2. Sports—Fiction. 3. Alligators—Fiction. 4. Humorous stories.] I. Title.
PZ7.E1314Aav 2015 [E]—dc23 2014012160

Printed in the United States of America

10 9 8 7 6 5 4 3 2 1

This book has been officially leveled by using the F&P Text Level Gradient™ Leveling System.

Random House Children's Books supports the First Amendment and celebrates the right to read.

STEP 1 READY TO READ

STEP INTO READING®

Aaron Is a Good Sport

by P. D. Eastman

Random House 🏠 New York

Walla Walla
County Libraries

This is Aaron.

Aaron is an alligator.

He likes to walk.

Aaron also likes
to run.

Look out!

Splat!

Aaron fell flat!

Aaron rides
a scooter.

It has two wheels.

He also rides a bike.
It also has
two wheels.

Aaron roller-skates, too.

Uh-oh!

Too many wheels!
Aaron falls down.

Aaron plays ball.

He throws.

He catches.

He throws the ball
again.

He catches the ball again.

He throws the ball
as hard as he can.

Uh-oh!

Aaron threw the ball
too hard!

"You broke my window!"

Aaron likes to garden.

He plants some seeds.

He waters the seeds.

He hopes they will
grow.

Aaron waits and waits.

He waters and waters.

Those seeds
sure did grow!

Aaron likes birds.

He sees a nest.

He pokes it
with a stick.

It is not a nest.

It is a bee hive!

Buzzzzzzz!

Uh-oh!

The bees do not like
Aaron.

Everything happens to Aaron!